I0699971

A TERROR TRIPTYCH

Disillusion · Insanity · Death

Kasey-Fallon

Querido ~ because without you, this book would not be.

Mas que todo.

Nenna ~ I didn't want to do this without you. But I hope you

see this, and every book after.

Contents

The Sleepover

They weren't welcome

Yet took over the island;

Made natives succumb

In the here and now

Several hundred years later

There's one who won't bow

"Missing" took up most of the flyer Brian had stopped walking to read at the stone pillars of the cemetery entrance. It had a picture of a young Asian girl with long, dark hair. Her smile was wide, and he could tell she was older than him by a bunch, but younger than his parents. Only a few weeks in at Canela High School, and this was the fifth missing poster he'd seen around town. With a shrug, he adjusted his backpack and walked on.

Maybe the kids at school would know more about all the missing people, Brian thought, shifting his backpack. His bag was mostly empty for now; the only thing he cared about was his sketchbook, weighing the heaviest on his shoulders. He would have liked to stop and sketch then, he thought, as he passed the cemetery. Only a block from his house, his walk to and from school took him past it every day, and the trees were really cool looking. Tall and almost bare towards the ground, they reached straight up and swayed with the wind. Although the bark looked grey, spears of deep green sprouted from limbs towards the top. With a small sigh, he walked on.

Being thirteen and an only child was rough, but moving from their farm in Ohio to some island so his parents could open a restaurant? That sucked. It wasn't even a *cool* island, like the one in Jurassic Park or the one with all the sea turtles. This place had no boardwalk, no cool rides like the one time they went on vacation to New Jersey, and there was *nothing* to do. Except surf, he thought, as his brow scrunched. He'd never learned how to swim, but he'd never told anyone. Being the new kid was bad enough, but being a teenager who couldn't swim was just embarrassing. As his gaze drifted over the headstones again, he wished for *anything* to do with friends.

As he rounded the corner to the last few blocks to school, a car zipped by with music blaring and kids screaming. *The Williams,* he thought a bit wistfully. One of the oldest and biggest families on the island, there were six kids and multiple cousins that he knew of. The ones in high school dropped the ones off in middle school first. They were all loud, outgoing, and happy... and made him feel like even more of an outsider just by existing.

Fourth period was his lunch, and this school was so much smaller than his school in Ohio, there were only two time blocks for it. The younger kids mostly got fourth period, while the older kids ate during fifth. He still didn't have any real friends, so he sat at different tables every fourth period wherever there was an empty seat.

During his first few days, everyone had asked him lots of questions - about his family, about the restaurant, and what it was like living landlocked in 'the states'. As soon as the curiosity wore off, the only people he spoke to were his teachers and the librarian, Mrs. Xavier, when he was checking out art books.

He leafed through his newest art book at the lunch table, absorbed in the indigenous people of the island and their art. Taino art was mostly little sculptures and designs on rock, it looked like, with lots of different symbols. He liked the abstract ones the most, and was busy sketching a few of his favorites into his sketchbook when a voice said next to him, "Hey, that's a pretty good Zemi."

Startled, Brian dropped his pencil. Surprised anyone was talking to him, he only stared at the tan boy with large, dark eyes. "A what?"

"A Zemi - it was like a god to us Tainos, a long time ago."

From his seat looking up, the boy was backlit with sun, which outlined his thin frame and spiky black hair. Brian noticed the boy's accent was different from most of the other students, but didn't want to point it out. "Oh," he said, looking back down at the drawing. "Thanks. I just started."

"I'm Ray," said the boy, sitting down next to him. "Ray Guayaba."

That made sense, Brian thought. *He must be old-school local.*

"Brian," he said, putting out his fist for a knuckle bump, which Ray only stared at with a small smile. "So you're from here?" he asked, awkwardly dropping his fist and picking his pencil back up.

"My family has a long history here."

"Cool."

"Where are you from?" Ray asked, watching Brian's pencil add detail to the Zemi's eye sockets.

"North America," he said. He'd learned that kids here stared at him blankly when he said 'Ohio'. Focused on his sketch with his shaggy hair falling over his eyes, he didn't notice Ray staring at him intently.

"Do you come from good people?"

Brian shrugged, feeling a little awkward. It was a weird thing to ask. "My parents are cool, I guess. My dad's a chef and my mom trains dogs."

Ray smiled. "I like dogs. I had a dog once. Coca - we named him for the leaves?" Brian nodded, with no idea what coca leaves were. "He was very crazy, but he gave us a lot of happiness."

"Cool. So how come I haven't seen you around before?" Brian asked, turning the pages of his book. Ray shrugged.

"I have not been in school for a while."

"Oh. Are you okay?" he asked. Maybe his new might-be-friend was sick or something. Ray smiled again, and stood up from the chair, with sunlight coming from the doorway making his eyes very dark, and glinting blueish off his black hair. "I am feeling much better than I was, thank you."

The bell rang, and all at once, Brian was surrounded by kids running out the door. Ray went with them, and Brian stood to go, hitting a girl with his backpack as he swung it over his shoulder. The weight of his books made a heavy *thwack* against her shoulder.

"Oh god, I'm so sorry." Brian said, putting his bag down.

"Jeez, what do you have in there, bricks?" said the girl, rubbing her shoulder.

"Some heavy books. I'm really sorry."

"It's okay. Hey, aren't you in my history class next?"

"I think so," he said, squinting at her sideways as they left the cafeteria. He sat in the back in history, mostly with his head down, so he wasn't sure.

"Did you do okay on the quiz? I failed. I'm pretty sure Miss. Moran hates me," she said with a grin.

He grinned back. His second conversation in one day! "Yeah, I did okay. I got an eighty-something."

"Oh, do you think I could get your notes?"

"Sure."

"Okay. Sit with me at lunch tomorrow?"

"Sure."

She hesitated before they walked into Miss. Moran's class. "Do you ever say anything else?"

"Sure," he said, just to make her laugh. "I'm Brian, by the way."

"Lottie Williams," she said, and preceded him into the room just as the bell rang.

He didn't see Ray again for the rest of the day, but Lottie waved at him as he left school. The graveyard looked so picturesque in the afternoon light; he decided to walk through it instead of the two blocks around it.

As his eyes swept from tree to tree, he guessed he wouldn't have any 'traditional' fall anymore, even by an old cemetery; no changing leaves, no pumpkins, no chilly Halloweens or apple picking. His thoughts sent his mood south again, and he kicked at a rock, looking up when the rock hit hard against a tombstone. Wincing, he patted the tombstone as he walked past.

"Sorry." He didn't stop to read it, or see the name Guayaba glint in the sunlight.

The next day, he found Ray already in his history class when he walked in with Lottie. He sat at the back, alone, staring out the window. Brian took the seat next to him.

"Ray, hi! I didn't know you were in this class."

Ray shrugged and twirled a pencil in one hand as he gave Brian a small smile. "I am now."

During class, Brian noticed Ray took no notes, but knew the answers to every question the teacher asked. He twirled his pencil and Brian couldn't help but admire his casual attitude. He was just so *cool.* When the bell rang, Brian turned to Ray but before he could speak, Lottie popped up at his desk with a few friends in tow.

"Guys, this is Brian. He's from the mainland, but he's cool, so be nice," she said with a little smile. Brian felt his chest pounding as he blushed. He didn't notice Ray quietly fade back and leave the room.

Ray caught up with Brian leaving school, saying he lived that way too. "This graveyard is only fifty years old or so," Ray said as they walked between the low stone pillars. "The island decided they wanted to give the proper respect to the Taino people. They even moved many of our graves here."

Brian shuddered as Ray said 'our graves'; he knew everyone died eventually, but it was just creepy to hear a kid talk about having a grave like that. Ray's disgust for the graveyard was obvious. "But isn't that a good thing?" Brian asked

With a huff, Ray picked up a stick and sent it flying. "How do you give something to someone after you have stolen it from them?" He walked up to a large tombstone emblazoned with Guayaba and Brian winced, remembering hitting it with a rock.

"Before the settlers came, my people had a wonderful way of life. They fished, they prayed, they celebrated life... they were slaughtered, so many of them. Many fell sick to the diseases the settlers brought, and the rest were thrown into poverty, or turned into servants."

Brian didn't know what to say. "I'm sorry Ray. At least there's good people here now..." he trailed off as a crack of lightning lit the sky, followed moments later by an echoing boom. Ray was still staring at the tombstone and sighed.

"Are there a lot of crazy storms here?" Brian asked, looking up at the darkening sky. A small smile hovered over Ray's mouth.

"There are many storms here, my friend. One is certainly coming."

Over the next few weeks, Brian fell into a pattern; during lunch, he sat with Lottie and her friends, and after school he walked home with Ray. Lottie brought Ray up one afternoon next to his locker.

"How come you hang out with that kid?" she asked, staring at him as he switched out books. He shrugged, uncomfortable knowing that his two best friends didn't like each other.

"It's cool that you're nice to him, it's just..." Lottie trailed off, hesitating.

"Just what?" he asked, zipping up his backpack.

"Nobody really knows who he is. No one knows where he came from or where he lives. He's just... here sometimes."

Brian remembered what Ray had told him when they first met. He could relate; kids in Ohio frequently missed some school to help with family farms or harvesting. "Maybe his family needs him or something, so he has to miss school."

"Maybe." Lottie said, clearly unhappy with that explanation. "He's just so *weird!* Nobody wants to talk to him."

Brian slammed his locker shut. Ray had been the first person to actually show an interest in him and start talking to him. "Well, how is anyone supposed to get to know him if no one even talks to him?"

Lottie stepped back, surprised. She opened her mouth to reply, but the bell rang and he stepped back from his locker, walking away without another word. Neither of them saw Ray standing in the shadow of an open door, smiling.

"So, what do you like to do?" Ray asked, throwing and catching a baseball as they walked.

Brian shrugged. His conversation with Lottie was playing back through his head on repeat. "I don't know. I sketch."

Ray stopped throwing to look at him. "Sketch?" His pronunciation of the word sketch sounded more like skesh.

"I draw. Like the day we met." Ray nodded and continued throwing.

"Do you think you could sketch me a picture, Brian?" Ray asked. Brian perked up at the idea.

"Of course! What kind of picture?"

"It is an old design of my people. Two Zemis, in a cemetery?" Ray stopped throwing the ball to look at Brian. Brian took his sketch pad out of his backpack and started a quick outline. Ray continued, "With light coming from above, out of the clouds, and some symbols on the graves? I can give them to you tomorrow."

Brian thought it was a little creepy, but nodded. After stowing his pad away, they continued their slow walk through the tombstones. The questions resumed.

"Do you have a favorite holiday?"

"Christmas."

Ray twisted his lips, and Brian figured maybe they didn't celebrate Christmas here as much. He didn't want to insult Ray. He wasn't sure what kind of religion the Tainos were, but he was kind of doubting they celebrated Christmas.

"But it might change, I guess," Brian rushed on, "since Christmas probably isn't the same without pine trees and snow and everything."

Ray nodded. "What do you like to eat?" he asked, as Brian was looking up at the trees around the cemetery.

"Huh?" The questions had been nonstop since they'd started walking, and Brian was thinking maybe Lottie was right. Maybe Ray was just weird.

"I'm sorry. I have offended you?" Ray asked, rolling the baseball around in his hands. "I do not... talk to many people. I do not have a lot of friends, like you." Brian shook his head. Of course he was going to be awkward; he wasn't used to having normal conversations.

"No, it's okay, um... I really miss deep-dish pizza, from the States. The only pizza you guys have here is frozen." Brian said, laughing.

"Pizza..." Ray said, gazing out over the tombstones. "I have seen it, but I have never had it."

"What?!" Brian shouted. No way could he be a good friend and let that go. "I'll have to bring you some. We can have it at lunch one day."

Ray smiled a little as the breeze ruffled his black hair. "You are kind. But I have... stomach problems? I cannot eat many things. But thank you."

Brian sighed and kept walking. "Okay. But if you can ever have it, pizza is great."

"Oh, I'm sure I will. One day." Ray stared hard around at the graveyard, and the hair at the base of Brian's neck rose. Brian didn't know what to say. The mood had shifted, and he wasn't sure what had made Ray angry again.

"I should probably get home," he said, stepping back quietly. Ray didn't turn or say goodbye, but let out a small laugh.

"Yes. Go back to your family. Enjoy it. While you still have one." His voice had turned harsh, and his eyes glared speculatively at Brian from beneath dark lashes.

Confused and spooked, Brian turned and hurried from the rows of silent death while clouds rolled in. That's what made him creeped out, he thought. He must have felt the air pressure change because of the storm. But that didn't explain Ray acting like a psycho... he looked back and saw the graveyard was empty. Ray was gone.

Avoiding Ray for the rest of the week was easy, particularly since Brian started avoiding the cemetery and getting rides from the Williams. He couldn't figure out what Ray's *problem* was. It wasn't as if *they* had done anything to the Tainos, or Guayabas, or whoever. The more he thought about it, the better Brian felt about avoiding him.

He saw Ray on Friday, probably waiting for him after school at the bottom of the stairs, throwing his beat up baseball into the air over and over. With a quick pivot, Brian used the side stairs instead of the front and blended in with the crowd. Maybe he had some anger issues or needed therapy, Brian thought as he lowered his head. But that didn't mean it had to be his problem.

"Brian, hey!" Lottie called from the top of the stairs. Ray *must* have heard her, but he turned and waved up at her, studiously ignoring where Ray stood.

"Do you have anything going on this weekend?" she asked, a little out of breath from jogging down to him. The morning after their argument at his locker, she'd shyly apologized for being judgemental. Since he hadn't been spending time with Ray, she'd been hanging out with him all week.

"I have to check with my parents, but I don't think so. What's up?"

"A bunch of us are going to the beach together. I wanted to see if you wanted to come?" He thought about telling her his embarrassing secret, but just before he opened his mouth, one of Lottie's older brothers walked up.

"Is this the guy?" he asked, curling a protective arm around Lottie. She nodded, smiling a little. It was obvious she'd mentioned him to her family, more than just giving another random kid a ride from school. The thought made Brian blush.

"I don't get in the water much," he admitted, shifting his backpack.

"I have a board you can use. We'll pick you up around seven?" Brian kissed his dreams of sleeping in goodbye, but nodded sure, as long as it was okay with his parents. He would text Lottie later.

"Tell them we're taking you to one of the safest beaches, okay?" said her brother, leading Lottie away. "Nobody disappears at this one!"

With his brow wrinkled in thought, *nobody disappears… at this one?* Brian turned for home. After a brief glance to the other side of the school's staircase, he saw Ray was nowhere in sight. Still, he walked around the outside of the cemetery, just in case.

Seven a.m. came early after staying up late texting with Lottie, and Brian was blinking from behind his sunglasses as they approached the beach. The glare of the sun was compounded by its sparkle off the water, but even half asleep he could admit it was beautiful.

"Not bad for someplace you never wanted to live, huh?" asked Lottie, plopping down beside him after leaving the water.

"I never said I didn't want to live here," he said, a little defensive. She laughed.

"You didn't have to. You were miserable when you first came here."

He winced, remembering exactly how miserable he'd been. "Yeah, maybe. But it's not that this place isn't great."

"There's literally no place else I'd want to be," she said, putting her sunglasses back on and picking up an apple. "Do you want to come out yet? You said you would once you woke up, and you've been sitting here for like an hour." He hesitated. "There are no sharks or anything."

"Look, if I tell you something, will you keep it a secret?" Eyes wide, she set her apple down and nodded. Brian sighed and said, "I never learned how to swim."

"What?!" she yelled. Shushing her, he leaned in closer.

"What happened to keeping it a secret? It's just - I lived in the *middle* of America, okay? We didn't have a pool, and it really never came up."

She thought about it, crunching her apple again, and then offered it to him. "Okay. I'll teach you. I've never met someone who couldn't swim. Living here, it seems like that's one of the first things they teach us. It's like the island's baptism. Everyone just gets thrown in the water." He laughed, and she joined in. "But you have to come in now, at least up to your waist, or it'll be too obvious. I'll get everyone to play volleyball or something, so you can stay where it's shallow."

"Okay," he said, and stood up, leaving the naked core on his towel. She reached for his hand and he thought he'd never felt happier.

As they reached the water's edge, Brian felt an itch between his shoulders. He looked around, certain someone was watching him. Seeing no one, he chalked it up to nerves from the water, and waded in.

At the edge of the trees, Ray stood just behind the treeline. In the shadows, he watched, and in the darkness, he planned.

The next day, Brian woke up to birdsong. On such a beautiful morning, he wanted nothing more than to go sketch the trees from the cemetery. If Ray was there, he thought, shouldering his backpack, he'd just go sit someplace else.

There was no one there, at least not at first. He made himself comfortable backed up against a tall tree. As the sun rose higher in the sky and the light shifted coming through the trees, Ray came up to him. Brian wasn't surprised; he'd seen him coming and decided if they had a problem, then *Ray* could leave. What *was* a surprise was the bag of pizza combos Ray tossed in his lap.

"It was the best I could do, and I wanted to apologize."

Brian said nothing, but opened the bag, took a few and after a minute, offered it to Ray. Ray shook his head, but sat down beside him at the base of the tree, facing away from him. Neither said anything for a while, and Brian continued his sketch.

Ray started speaking softly. "I was raised by my grandparents. My mother passed several years ago, and they took me in. Their parents are gone, but they worked for the Williams, a long time ago. They were a proud people, but to the Williams they were just servants, do you understand?" He asked, but continued without waiting for Brian to reply.

"They were treated poorly, and my family never forgot. But it is hard to find work on this island, that is not working for the Williams in some way. My grandfather just passed away, and I have not been myself. I am sorry I was harsh."

Brian wasn't sure what to say. Ray continued.

"In two weeks, it will be a celebration, yes? Your Halloween?" Brian nodded. "I have seen that your Halloween is when people enjoy cemeteries. The day after is my people's day to honor the dead. We could celebrate? Spend the night in the cemetery?"

Brian hesitated in surprise. Spending time under pretty trees during the day was one thing, but staying overnight?

"I'm not sure my parents will-" Ray cut him off.

"Don't you live right there?" he asked, pointing down the block to where Brian could *just* see the light blue of their house.

"Yeah," he said, still thinking. His dad probably had their old tent somewhere.

After another minute of quiet, Ray added with a small hopeful smile, "And your Halloween is my birthday as well." It decided him.

"Okay," he said, turning back to his sketch of trees. "As long as my parents say it's okay. I think we have a tent we could use."

A fist appeared slowly in front of Brian's sketch, and he was happy to finally knuckle bump Ray. Smiling, Ray said he'd see Brian at school, and walked back from the way he'd come in. A little while later, Brian realized he couldn't feel his tailbone anymore, so he turned to get up and froze.

The other side of the tree had a bald spot at its base where the grass had turned brown and brittle. The bark on that side of the tree was grey and brittle compared to where he'd been sitting.

He was sure it hadn't looked like that when he'd gotten there. What was worse was the small dead bird at the edge of browned grass that Brian reached for automatically. Just before touching it, he hesitated. There was nothing he could do for it, and it might have a disease or something. He grabbed his backpack quickly and looked up into the tree for any kind of nest where the bird might have fallen from. There was nothing.

Slightly nauseous, he left, and was almost home before it hit him. That was where Ray had been sitting.

<hr>

After lunch later that week, Ray reminded Brian of the sketch he wanted of the cemetery. As they sat at the back of the room, Brian added details to the trees and shadowed the backs of the headstones. He passed it to Ray, who smiled, then scribbled a note and handed it back to Brian with the picture.

He couldn't make sense of the symbols, but Brian guessed it was Taino. Ray's note said to-

"Gentlemen! I hope we're not disturbing you, but we have class going on here," said Miss. Moran from the front of the room. Scowling at both of them, she nodded approval at their silence and said, "No more passing notes in my class," before turning back to the whiteboard at the front.

Brian had shifted his class notebook in front of the sketch until a few moments later, Ray tossed another sheet of paper on his desk. With a grin, Brian wrote out **of course** in response to Ray's **can you finish it?** He pretended to take notes on the Byzantine Empire while adding more of the symbols to Ray's picture. In the middle of handing it back to

Ray, Miss. Moran spotted them. Ray didn't move a muscle, but Brian jumped almost out of his skin when she started yelling.

"Detention! All week! You'll be helping my history club clean out the basement! Maybe you'll learn that those who don't pay attention to history really *are* doomed."

That afternoon, Brian had to agree with Miss. Moran. His shoulders ached from hauling boxes around the basement, and his eyes were watering from sneezing so much. Dust covered everything, muting colors into grey, so that the basement felt like they'd stepped into an old black and white movie. Ray didn't seem to have the same issues he was, moving boxes silently without complaint. Brian envied him a little.

After they'd organized everything according to Miss. Moran, she gave each of them boxes to sort through. "Any pictures you come across are gold boys. I want them organized into school pictures, town pictures, and Indigenous pictures." She hesitated slightly over the word Indigenous as Ray looked up at her with a flat gaze. With a last look at Ray she fled the room, and Brian shook his head, opening a box.

His latest box was mostly old photos, so he took his time sorting, even enjoying going through them. When he was almost at the back of the box, a black and white class photo caught his eye. The front of the school was bright white, and Brian guessed it had been built recently. It looked the same from the street as he walked up every day, and he thought it was cool they had kept the original building. The class itself wasn't particularly interesting; a small huddle of maybe twenty kids and a teacher in a floor-length grey dress.

But one boy stood apart from the group; he was lean, with black hair and dark eyes. Brian wasn't aware he'd been holding his breath until he expelled it all in a whoosh as Ray asked from next to him, "Find something interesting?"

Brian jolted and shuffled the picture in with the rest. "No, just a lot of old pictures. I think my eyes are getting tired though," he said with a laugh, rubbing his eyes. Another hour passed and Miss. Moran came to tell them their detention was over for the day; she'd see them tomorrow.

The fresh air felt wonderful after being in the basement for hours, and Brian breathed it in greedily. He could just smell the ocean; he'd gotten used to smelling it on the breeze, and now he enjoyed it as they started their walk through the cemetery.

"Ray?" Brian asked. The old picture shifted in his mind.

"Yes, Brian?" Brian smiled. Ray was always so... proper.

"Did you have any relatives go to our school?" Ray didn't answer at first, and looking over Brian saw him gazing up at the clouds as the sun lowered in the sky.

"It is possible," Ray said at last. "I know my family would not have had much time to attend school, but perhaps for a few years. Why?"

"Oh, yeah, that explains it," Brian said. "One of the old pictures back there, there's this kid that looks a lot like you."

Brian missed the sharp look Ray gave him, looking up at the beginning of sunset now himself. From down the block, he heard a voice.

"Brian Regan Hanover! Detention?!" she called, and they heard her clearly, although they were only partway through the cemetery. Brian blushed hard, hoping he wasn't about to be embarrassed.

He waved at his mother and turned to Ray - who was already halfway across the graveyard in the other direction. Confused, he wondered, *had he run? Why did he run away?* He brushed it off as he jogged towards his mother. Some teens had a thing about parents.

The day had finally come. Halloween. All day, Brian had wanted to talk to Ray about it, but Ray wasn't at school. His parents had agreed to a sleepover - *in the cemetery!* He knew it was only because his mother could see the cemetery from their front porch, but still. It was majorly cool of them.

As he checked his backpack for the third time, he rolled his eyes and zipped it shut. Obviously, if they forgot anything he could just run home. With the tent in a cylinder bag over his other shoulder, he made his way to the cemetery to wait for Ray.

Ray was already there, sitting in front of the Guayaba headstone. His expression was hard to make out since the sun was just setting on the far side of the island, but Brian could see his outline clearly defined by the little circle of candles he'd lit. Almost in black and white, it was a little eerie, but Brian liked it. It was Halloween after all - what was Halloween without a little spooky?

"Hey man. What's up with the candles? Are those allowed in here?" Brian asked, stepping up to the circle.

Ray smiled and said, "They keep the bugs away." Brian nodded; of course. He'd never slept outdoors on an island before. Ray would know how to do it right.

"I think we'll be okay once we set the tent up, right?" Brian asked, placing the tent bag down next to the headstone.

"I wonder if you would like to sleep under the stars instead?" Ray asked. "It's a beautiful night, and the sky is so clear," he said, looking up. Brian stared up as well, and Ray was right. Thousands, no, *millions* of stars splayed across the sky. Constell-ations he'd never seen before made him feel small and awed. He wondered how he'd ever draw something like it.

"Yeah," Brian said, still gazing up. "The stars are cool." They settled in, and Brian brought out the sketch he'd finished for Ray. As soon as he saw it, Ray lit up.

"This is perfect," he said, setting it aside. "You really are a very good artist. Here." He passed Brian a hard leather pouch, bearing similar symbols as the picture. "Drink. It is a celebration drink."

Brian kicked the end of the pouch up and got a mouthful in before the fire hit his throat and he coughed. Ray laughed.

"Slowly, my friend. It has... tequila." Brian sipped this time, and didn't feel like his face was on fire. After another sip he handed it back and grabbed some snacks out of his backpack. Ray didn't eat any, but they passed the pouch back and forth. They leaned back against the headstone and stared up at the stars, speaking every now and again as the stars got brighter, and the sky deepened even more. Brian thought he might be drunk for the first time. He laid down inside their circle of candles on his small travel pillow.

He glanced over as Ray reached outside the circle and brought out a small box. The wooden box was simple, but covered in Taino markings. He recognized several from the drawing Ray had asked for.

"This was a gift from my grandmother," Ray said, opening the lid and bringing out a bumpy frog with darker spots. Brian smiled and looked back to the stars. .

"That's really nice Ray. Can it breathe okay in that box?" Brian finished the question on a yawn. He wondered idly what time it was, and if Ray wanted to go to sleep soon.

A strange, wet sound made Brian look back at Ray. He now held the frog's body, twitching. Confused, he found the frog's head; it lay in the dirt at Ray's feet. Ray was using a finger to smear the frog's blood across his own forehead, and Brian could only watch in shock as he reached across to draw on Brian's as well.

The blood felt sticky, but it was the scent that turned Brian's stomach. The frog's legs were still trying to escape Ray's hand. Brian felt the same as he tried to scramble back from Ray. He could barely move. Ray began to chant.

Beyond fuzzy, Brian felt lightheaded, like a permanent sense of going over hills in a car too fast. His extremities were tingling, and the whites of Ray's eyes had been overtaken with black. Brian could only stare up in horror.

"What are you doing?" he whispered, trying to creep away from the boy. Focused on his chanting, Ray didn't spare Brian much of a look, and sighed.

"You are probably a good boy, Brian," he says, and his voice has deepened, his accent even stronger. "A part of me is sorry this is the way it has to be, but that will not stop me. Not again." Brian's brow twisted as his confusion ran across his face.

"That picture you found? It was 1942, and the schoolhouse was new. I impersonated this child you see before you. He died of the influenza and poor care. The white doctors would not treat him. He was tossed into a mass grave in the woods, with so many of our people. I tried to recreate what I had once seen the spirit masters of Vodou achieve. They brought one of their spirit leaders to life, in the body of another."

As he spoke, Brian's eyes drifted half closed as though he were tired. He fought it and forced them back open. His brain was screaming for him to run away, but he heard it dimly, through the heavy sense of weightlessness throughout his body.

Ray chanted another verse of words and continued his story. "Our teacher, I thought, was a suitable vessel. But her spirit was… impure, perhaps? The change did not take, and her body died around me after only hours. It took me a long time to visit this world again; to make you see me as this boy. To influence the teachers I was just another student who belonged." He shook his head, frowning. "But my power is erratic. I cause storms, and the power seeps out of me into my surroundings. I need a new vessel, Brian. I need you."

Brian's lips were so numb he wasn't sure his mouth was moving, but he heard himself whisper, "For what?"

Ray looked at him fully, considering how to answer. His black eyes glinted in the candlelight before he bowed his head, bringing his hand to his chest. "I was once called Maquetaurie Guayaba, and my people believed in me."

He smiled then, and Brian's whole body got chills. This was no boy's smile; no human smile. The teeth were too pronounced, and the mouth was now too wide for Ray's face. He continued, "I am the God of Death."

"Without the belief of my people, it has taken me centuries to walk here among you. To speak as you do, and to move objects... It has been a significant task. I will wreak vengeance upon this island that turned against its people. No more will we be forgotten!" His hand slashed across the air as he spoke. "No more mass graves across the island, or in the woods, to be made pretty with flowers in this falsehood of respect."

Brian rolled his eyes around the cemetery, looking for help. It was Halloween, right? Surely *some* people would be out? Ray noticed and shook his head.

"No one is coming, boy. Even in this century, this night is the first night of All Souls. People will be at home, staying with their families. People will come out tomorrow to honor their ancestors at these graves and find only me."

Brian's body felt like it had fallen asleep, but the anger he felt was stronger. With a shout, he flung his backpack by its strap at Ray. The books inside made a sickly satisfying smack against Ray's head, knocking him to the ground. With an inhuman growl, Ray picked up the backpack, and Brian watched in shock as it turned to ash.

Laying on his side now, Brian panted for air as he suddenly realized he was about to die. Tears fell from his eyes, running across his face. The wet tracks caught the candlelight, and Ray noticed. He sighed and stood up, stretching his chest and shoulders in a way no human could.

"I am sorry, Brian. You have been a good friend."

Brian sniffled. "Will it hurt?"

The god posing as a boy paused. "I do not think so. It did not hurt the teacher or the girl I once witnessed. They simply fell asleep. In a way, it is very much like your natural death, and your spirit will go on its way."

"Wha-what will you do?" Brian managed, though he was so cold his teeth were chattering. Ray was right, he thought. It didn't really hurt. This time Ray did not hesitate, but smiled viciously.

"I have studied your human ways. Your Lottie? She will be my key. With her I will unlock the doors to the Williams. Eventually, I will marry her and destroy the family empire. I will destroy this island as it stands and rebuild the faith that was taken from me."

Done explaining, Ray closed his eyes and placed Brian's drawing between them. It was sandwiched between Brian's hand and his own below it. Brian could see where it was splattered with blood as Ray started chanting.

Brian closed his eyes and in a burst of light he saw it all - the crossing of Ray's spirit into him. There was Ray, talking, laughing and smiling at his own parents on Christmas. Lottie was kissing him behind the school, and he held her hand as they walked. He felt himself get down on one knee and heard her squeal before the vision dissolved into so many others.

The Williams' homestead was on fire; townspeople were rioting; there was a computer screen with numbers counting down. He felt the rush of blood as he slit Lottie's throat and felt nothing but pleasure; he heard himself making speeches, shaking hands, and signing paperwork. It was true, all of it. Ray would make it come true… using *his* body.

With a last tug, Brian felt a floating and a separation as he watched his own body from the side.

His body's eyes were pouring light, and the vision of Ray was wavering. He continued chanting, crouched on the ground. The light coming from his eyes passed through Ray as Brian floated. He was shifting away from the scene, and in stark contrast to just moments ago, he felt a remote apathy. The vision was getting darker in front of him, but it was bright all around him as his spirit drifted, weightless.

As he shifted away from what he used to be, he felt a magnetic pull - downward. He was being pulled down into the ground, much faster than he'd been pushed out of his body. He flung his hands out, grasping for anything, and as one hand found his own body, he clutched on to the ankle.

With everything Brian had, he focused on holding tight. He watched, his spirit burning brightly, as Ray's eyes - his own eyes - darkened, and went from glowing light to black. Lit with an inner fire, the blackness glowed briefly. As if Ray had flexed, Brian felt Ray's incredible power surge outward in a ripple and flow through him. He held on even tighter. Feeling victory, Ray sat up and noticed Brian still at his feet, clutching.

From inside Brian's body, Ray frowned. "I do not understand. You should have gone up into the afterlife. Crossed over." He kicked his physical foot, almost dislodging Brian's grip. Brian focused on nothing else and closed his eyes. The pull from below was getting stronger, but he refused to let go. He thought of his parents - of Lottie - of never learning how to swim - of pizza - of this pretty island, no matter how much death it held. He could not let Ray win.

Brian felt a lurch; a shift, and opened his eyes to see the vision of Ray superimposed over his own body. The bodies merged, then separated, over and over again in a strobe like effect. Brian's spirit was slowly sinking below the ground, and still he held on, until the only thing above the cemetery's grass was his head and one arm, nearly fused to Ray's ankle.

Brian's body jolted one last time, and falling back to the ground it expelled Ray on impact. With a shriek of rage, Ray reached for Brian. Now that nothing held them above ground, Brian felt the pull over his whole being as they were drawn downward. The stop was so sudden he was jostled into letting go of Ray, who hit the floor of the coffin a moment after him. Ray had made claw marks in the dirt on the way down, and Brian watched with fascination as the marks disappeared, slowly being filled in with dirt. He could just see up through the ground for a moment, and knew he was seeing those millions of stars for the very last time.

Just past dawn, the first to find Brian's body was a runner, and her scream was endless. It ricocheted across the island, careening past the headstones and their secrets. It floated into the trees that held such horrors, and along the shoreline, finally swallowed and silenced by the waves.

The
Visitor

With pulsing, pleading, heart-pounding shakes
Night after night, I lie here awake
I meant it, I promised I would not break
If only for my sister's sake

But every moment of every day I fake
I try not to make those same mistakes
As this madness prowls like a thief and takes
Each vestige of peace I've tried to make

So I breathe through the mess as I wait and quake
Waiting for light that comes with dawn's break
I clench my jaw harder despite the ache
I'm not sure how much more of this I can take

Before the monster inside starts to partake
In this flimsy charade; the sanity I retake
Every day; every layer of this world I remake

…if only for my sister's sake.

My sister was having one of her bad days… this was one of the worst I'd ever seen. My eyes continued their small-scale assessment of what I held, sounding out bass-sih-tray-sin different ways in my mind. I wondered who had created it, and what for. Where they were now; likely maggot food, where no amount of ointment would help. I believe I found that hilarious that day. My dark sense of humor readied me to look beyond the tube of ointment in my hands. The floor, worn linoleum in enormous squares, was an indecipherable pattern of splotches. I supposed if they ever ran out of ink blots here they could just use the floor. The lights glared, illuminating everything no one wanted seen. But that was what these places were for; putting a spotlight on the darkness. I was just sick of everything being literal.

Windowsills weren't perches to sit and gaze at the outside; mirrors weren't to be called portals to another world, no matter how much Through the Looking Glass they played during lunch, and magazine racks weren't ladders for midgets. No one told jokes here, and it seemed like such a wasted opportunity. I looked at my sister, who'd faced away from me, and sat rocking at the edge of the bed. Her hospital given shift was purple and only seemed to make the bags under her eyes more stark against her sun-deprived skin.

I rubbed her shoulder for a moment before trying to turn her my way; she wouldn't budge, and only burrowed her head deeper into the thin blanket wrapped around her shoulders. So I sat behind her and shifted so I was looking at her in the mirror. She'd been here long enough without incident that she'd been given a room with a mirror. Well. A sort of mirror. It was highly polished something-or-other, but apparently wouldn't break. Sighing, I reached out to brush at the ends of her hair where it sat messily at her neck.

"It doesn't matter," I said, softly enough that at first I wasn't sure she'd heard me. "It doesn't matter." I repeated, stronger.

"Of course it matters." She said, in between hiccuping, teary breaths.

"It'll grow back."

"*When?*" she asked, finally looking at me with tear-filled doe eyes in the not-mirror. The mirror had an odd, almost curved funhouse effect, and made her eyes even bigger for a moment; her nose even smaller. I wish I could say the funhouse was amusing, but it was only grotesque.

"Just as soon as you stop taking it off, I expect." I said, being sure to look her straight in the eyes and not let my gaze wander.

She gave a half laugh, and fell into my lap, crying full out. My tears fell silently into her dark, choppy hair. I breathed through it, letting the air escape so slowly it didn't make a sound. By the time she'd sat back up my eyes were dry, and she grinned.

"Want to color?" she asked, as if the tears had never been. I smiled and looked her straight in the eyes.

"Of course I do. I even brought new markers." Markers were allowed, so long as the door stayed open, and someone at the check-in desk counted them on the way in, and again on the way back out. I'd learned people used markers for makeshift weapons. No matter how long I stared at the markers, I couldn't see it. I suppose that was why I wasn't dressed in a purple gown.

Giddy with excitement, she knelt up on the bed, knocking the ill-topped bacitracin to the floor. Crouching down, I grabbed for it and saw a shadow sway under the bed. Glancing up, I saw my sister sat exactly as she'd been a moment ago, looking at me expectantly. Not wanting her to think I was staring, I looked back under the bed… nothing.

I sighed at the effect the fluorescent lights had on my eyes. I placed the little tube on her plastic, cornerless nightstand and rifled through my bag. As my hand closed around the markers the bed creaked, and I looked back to see she still hadn't moved, but was staring into middle distance, making shapes with her mouth. I popped my lips, and she looked up at me, smiling. We traded pops and whizzes for several moments before she got bored and went to the door. She stopped once she got to the doorway, and looked back at me, markers in hand.

The lighting was a little softer coming from the hallway, and it was then I was able to look at her face and not need to scream. As much. I stared at her shredded cheekbones and forehead in the reflection of the door's window. Ribbons of red merged with pits of scabby blackness, and some pieces of skin glistened. Harsh marks sat at her neck as raw, unwelcome necklaces. Whether the gleam was from the medical gel, or fresh bursts of blood or pus I couldn't tell. She'd spent a decent amount of time over the last day or so peeling the skin off her own face. That afternoon alone I'd spent almost an hour following her around so I could put bacitracin on the gouges. She refused to sit still long enough for me to treat all the wounds. She reminded me of a panicked bird newly captured.

The staff had sedated her, treated the wounds, clipped her nails as much as possible, and called me. She was on stronger medication now than she'd been in several years, and she'd been nodding off to sleep when I came in. They told me they didn't know what had caused the mental break; she'd been doing so well, it was in all the doctor's notes. I'd seen them, writing their notes as they spied on us. They attempted to be unobtrusive but they ruined our times together.

I shook it off, and she held out her hand to walk with me. She'd been institutionalized so long ago it felt like, and now waited at every door for permission to go through, like a well-trained dog. I didn't notice until we were halfway down the hall to the Rec Area that I'd heard that soft creak again on our way out.

The coloring session went well enough. I colored an intricate garden mandala design, which she thought was boring, as she colored large tropical birds in trees. I remembered coloring as a small child with our mother. I couldn't remember the last time I'd seen her…

I shook my head at the vague memory, and looked over to see my sister staring out the window as the sun slid down in the sky. It was late, this time of year in August. I couldn't recall the last time she'd seen a sunset out in the world, and I sketched one for her. I flipped over my page, quickly bringing a sunset to life over a beach. I put a thick stand of trees around the beach, and for a moment I got a chill looking at the image. It reminded me of something… I couldn't place it.

I saw when I looked up that she was smiling at the picture, and asked me to sign it. I hated my signature, it just never *felt like me*, but I signed it to make her happy. Flipping the page over, I went to finish my mandala, except now I was looking down at tropical trees. Birds had glowing red eyes, and sharp talons dripping blood onto dense foliage. She'd covered the ground and space between the trees in fog and shadows. My heart thudded painfully in my chest, again pulling on a memory. This forest reminded me of another forest; one without birdsong.

I must have grabbed her page by accident to flip over and sketch on, but thankfully she didn't seem upset by it. I slid her page back across the table to her, and with a shaky breath retrieved my mandala page from where I'd pushed it aside.

"Darling, why are the birds angry?"

"They're not angry," she said, looking confused with a mar between her scabbed eyebrows. She kept coloring, and soon the leaves were not only spotted with red, but bleeding.

"Then why are their eyes red?"

"They're tropical of course."

"Oh." I let the silence rest a moment before asking, "Are your trees bleeding?"

"No... I think it's from the people in the trees," she said quietly, and I froze. I wasn't sure how to answer that. We continued coloring for a little while longer, but my heart wasn't in it. I couldn't look across the table to where red now ran down the trees as if sprayed from arteries. With my gut churning, I officially never wanted to visit the tropics. Well. Never again.

A nurse stopped by the table. I noticed she avoided looking at my sister's face at all when she said "Time's almost up here. Are you ready to clean up and head back?"

I nodded, collecting my markers. She counted them one by one as I slid them in their box. We stood and gathered our pages, and I glanced at the clock. It seemed like hours had passed since we'd sat to color. Night here looked no different from daytime, given the lighting, but now it was almost time for my sister to take her medicine and get some rest. We walked back towards the bedroom, and I recalled the squeak of the bed as we'd left. I needed to know what was making that groaning creak. It was giving me chills.

"Hey, let me go in first?" I asked her once we got to the door.

"Why? Is something wrong?" she blurted, her eyes going wide. Multiple co-occurring diagnoses seemed to mean she would react outrageously to a casual statement one day, then ignore it the next. It was always a fine line, not upsetting the both of us.

"No no," I assured, with a small smile, "I just…" the lie died on my lips. I didn't know what to say. I'd run out of non-upsetting statements. This would happen sometimes, at which point I knew it was time for me to go. "Stay here. I'm right through here, ok?"

She let me go through the door without another question, which was a blessing. The question days were the worst: why can't I have a belt or shoes, how come Thursday is spaghetti night, why are the trees evil, when are we leaving here? It was exhausting.

I entered the room and went straight to the bed, putting a knee down to peer under it. A mouse, perhaps…? Nothing moved. I stood and pressed down on the bed, trying to make the same squeal I'd heard earlier. With my hands on my hips I stared hard at the bed. I glanced up and frowned at the ceiling. Had there always been a hanging light in here?

A shadow came straight at me from the corner, jolting me from my contemplation. I would have sworn my heart stuttered and died. Which made it even more embarrassing as my sister clung to me and my heart started beating again. I blew out a long breath and paused to listen. She was mumbling about the trees, and creeping shadows, and how it wasn't her fault. It wasn't.

"What?" I asked, pushing her back a bit by the shoulders. She turned from me to face the window. I played with her hair and brushed it back from her face, careful not to touch the scratches.

We stared out the window and watched the shadows grow dark together. It had been a beautiful afternoon, but now all we saw was fog coming towards the hospital from the trees, and the trees themselves seemed to stretch on forever. I should have left by now.

"What wasn't your fault Darling? What didn't you do?"

"I didn't... I didn't take my face," she whispered. "It took my face, and it's wearing it. It wears my face and sways in the wind and thinks it's me. But it wasn't. It isn't. It's not me." Her voice was urgent, and her breath was stale; I leaned back.

"Okay," I whispered back, and closed my eyes. She couldn't take what she'd done to herself. I didn't want to, but I had to ask. "Who then? Who did it?"

She pulled away from me then, looking deep into my eyes, so big and brown like hers. "I thought it was you."

Stunned, I froze. She smiled then, pulling the scratches in her cheeks wide, splitting one open again on her right side. Casually, she rubbed the open mar and met my eyes in the window-turned-mirror, smearing the blood down to her jaw. The encroaching darkness had lengthened shadows, and I could feel them closing in. She asked "Is it time for bed? I'm a little tired."

Whirling away from the window, I faced back inside, only to be met with more darkness. Corners had turned into caverns, and the only light coming into the room was from the doorway. The hanging light had grown lower while we had our backs turned, and now hung halfway from the ceiling. It seemed to sway with the shadows. We heard the Nurses murmuring close by, and I quickly slapped at the light switch. It wouldn't help for long. A Nurse would come in any minute to turn it off, but for that minute the shadows slunk back to their confines.

As if my thoughts had summoned her, a Nurse walked in, soft grey shoes chirping every few steps. "It's time for your medicine," she told my sister, and I sat on the edge of the bed as she took her pills. It was never something I felt comfortable watching, and I think she felt the same. The Nurse nodded, and said "Lights out, dear. Two minutes."

I stood, hearing the low squeal again. It *had* to be the bed, but it didn't *sound like it came from the bed.* The noise echoed in my brain, resounding in a heavy toll. There was no time. I had to go. I reached for my bag, my hand grasping air at the floor. I looked around for it by the window. Perhaps I'd brought it out with me when we went to color. I would just pick it up on my way out. My sister had moved to the bed. She sat watching me. I stooped to kiss her on the cheek, but hesitated an inch away, aiming at the last second for an unmarred spot on her temple.

"I thought it didn't matter?" she whispered, gazing again into the middle of the room. She was looking at something I couldn't see.

"I just didn't want to hurt you," I said lowly, brushing her hair back again.

She turned to stare at me, never blinking, and I would swear she saw straight inside me. Right down to my soul, where sometimes I was afraid I was a little bit like her. I couldn't tear my gaze away.

"Then why did you take my face?" she said flatly.

The Nurse was back, saying sweet dreams. Another stood in the doorway smiling, cautiously glancing around the room before the lights went out on their timer. Not the light! The door snicked shut behind her, and the darkness rolled in. Shocked, I yelled.

"Wait, I'm still in here!" The solid door must have muted my voice. I strode to the door and flailed at the handle, willing it to turn, but it refused; we were locked in. Calling, knocking, I willed the Nurses on the other side of the door to hear. I jumped when I heard the damned creak. I pressed my back up against the door, looking around wildly. Layers of darkness surrounded me. The only thing I saw clearly of my sister was the large whites of her eyes, several feet above me. I whimpered. Her eyes bulged from the rope cinched tight around her neck, descending from the hanging light. I could hear that subtle creak again as her body swayed, left to right in front of me. Above me. The meager light glinted off the ointment on black pockets where her face should have been.

"The poor thing," I heard a Nurse say through the door as she walked away. "Went on vacation where her twin died or vanished or something. No one really knows what happened. Hasn't had a visitor in years."

The Copse

Walk here among us
Our dear little thing
Join in our chorus
Forever as we sing

Of all things beauty-
Fierce or tame
Riotous or soothing
You'll never be the
same

Once you're up in our
branches
We know you'll want to
stay
You won't need any
more chances
You'll stay with us, and
sway-

As smoothly as
moonlight
Drifts through our
leaves
Drift with us and take
flight
Like mist through the
breeze

Become one with the
forest
We know life's been so
hard
We offer you rest
And a lifelong reward

Of swaying in peace
No trying times ahead
All of this within reach
The sweet release of
the dead.

Tai wasn't sure he could make it. With the sun in his eyes, he licked his lips and tasted only salt. His heart pounded and although he was half submerged in water, he could feel the sweat pouring off him. He inhaled deep, twisted his hips and kicked his legs just in time to catch the barrel of the wave. He knew the instant his feet caught on the board and its layers of wax, and he felt the world drop away.

This. This is what it was to fly, he thought, directing the board with nature and physics. Water; salt; air; wax; gravity; wind; all rolled together as he soared towards the coast, until he dropped from the board to drift in. The bright yellow of the board was a perfect foil for the aquamarine waters off small Rumi Island. He heard his friends cheering him on from the beach. With a huge grin, he waved and figured that was his best wave of the day, and a good place to stop. Instead of soft sand, sharp shells and pebbles met his feet as he walked through the shallows. Wincing as he felt another small cut, he figured maybe this was why this beach - although great for waves - was almost empty.

"Tai!" Sonya rushed into the low waves and jumped up for a quick kiss. "That was awesome. How was it?"

"Great. I mean it's not the same as using your own board, and it's been a long time, but man that was cool. Where's Rob?" he asked, looking around.

"He said he had to get back to the marina, but he said you could bring the board back whenever."

"Yo Tai! I forgot you even surfed?!" James, one of his best friends all through college, shambled up to the water's edge, beer in hand.

"Haven't in like five years man, but I grew up surfing. California all the way." With a grin, he wrapped an arm around Sonya's shoulders and carried the borrowed surfboard under the other arm.

The other couple of their group, Shannon and Mariyah, were sitting with their shoes and towels. Sitting wasn't really accurate, he thought with an inner smile; they were just making out. They'd been together about as long as he and Sonya, but he thought they might last longer. They just seemed so… in tune.

As they approached the girls separated, but kept holding hands as they peered up. "You guys think we can head out soon?" asked Shannon, "I know I used sunscreen, but I'm still starting to burn." Sonya smirked a superior grin, and said "Sorry chica. You guys want to quit the beach for Shannon?" she asked, looking at the group.

Tai frowned; she'd made it sound like they had to leave because of Shannon, but they had all been ready to leave anyway. He said as much, and got a relieved little smile from Shannon while Sonya stepped away from him.

"Man, I'm starved. Didn't Rob say there's a little shop right around here?" James asked, looking around the empty beach. They all looked around;

while there had been a handful of people around earlier, the beach was now empty. Tai remembered that there weren't even any lifeguard stands, or flags to tell people what the riptides were, and it had been weirdly difficult to access. They'd had to walk over a half mile and then climb through and over rugged boulders between dense stands of trees to even get to the trail that led to the beach.

As he looked across the sand and into the trees in the silence, Tai heard whispers.

"What is that?" he asked, head cocking to the side. It seemed to come from all over, but when he closed his eyes to listen, it was coming from the trees.

"Rob told me the locals think this place is haunted," Sonya stated, rolling her eyes. "I mean obviously nobody comes here because of these freaking rocks."

"Don't you hear it?" Shannon said, eyes wide.

"I mean I hear something, but there's obviously nobody here." Sonya said with a hair flip. The group remained still for a minute, listening.

"I heard of this place, up in Maine, on the east coast? Where if you're quiet at these cliffs, they echo off the rocks and it sounds like thunder or clapping." James said.

Tai looked at him as James finished his beer. It could be something like that. "Yeah," he said nodding, "maybe there's a cave or something nearby that just echoes."

"Well Rob told us that that store has a little deli, with sandwiches and stuff?" said Shannon, standing to slap the sand off her bare legs. "He said it's through the trees to the right, but that we shouldn't go off the boardwalk. He said people get lost around here every year."

"Because people are stupid," Sonya said with another hair flip, adjusting her barely-there bikini top. Tai thought the breakup might be coming sooner rather than later.

As the group gathered their towels and made their way up the beach, Tai hung back, staring at the waves and listening to the whispers. It might be haunted, he figured, but it was still beautiful. Up the beach, the path took them back to the craggy boulders, where the trees pressed in from both sides. Tai thought it strange that he heard no birds, although the whispering was still faintly there. He heard the laughter from his friends ahead, and the swaying of branches, and nothing more. Instead of the salty ocean air, here under the canopy the air smelled stagnant, like layers of decay. Must be the leaves, he thought.

The trees shot straight up with a soft grey bark, and no low branches. Their slender boughs seemed to sway in tandem as he peered up. Haunted or not, he thought, it was definitely melancholy. Staring up, Tai didn't notice the fog that wound towards him, creeping with grasping tendrils.

Sonya shook his shoulder roughly. "Tai! What's wrong with you?"

He jolted, and dropped the surfboard that had sat loosely in his grip.

"What?" he asked.

"What are you looking at? I've been calling you for like ten minutes. I turned around and you were just gone."

He shook his head and picked the surfboard back up, switching arms. "Sorry, I guess I just zoned out. Surfing must have worn me out more than I thought." With a grin, he shook his head and blinked a few times. They continued up the path and reached the fork where the group waited on the wooden planks.

"You okay man?" asked James.

"Yeah, just spaced out for a minute. I must be beat. I need food!" With a high-five to James, he picked his way over the last of the larger rocks, surfboard in tow.

"Do you want to just leave that thing here?" asked Sonya. "You can just put it behind some rocks or something."

"I don't mind," said Tai, "I don't want anything to happen to it. Boards are expensive."

"There's nobody even here, it'll be fine," Sonya argued.

"Sonya, enough. It's not mine." he said, and started walking. The rest of the group fell in, awkwardly silent.

"So what kind of food do we think some rando deli-shop on a remote island even has?" James asked the group. Everyone chuckled, except Sonya, Tai noticed, but the tension eased.

"Ooh, I hope they have tropical smoothies," Shannon said, happily swinging her hand in Mariyah's. Tai looked over at Sonya, who was staring sullenly into the trees as they walked.

"What about tropical tacos?" James said. The girls laughed, and Tai joined in until he realized Sonya had fallen behind them. With a little sigh he held back and waited until she caught up.

"What's wrong?"

"Nothing," she pouted, staring into the canopy. She pulled back when he went to take her hand and they stopped on the narrow path.

"You never hold my hand anymore." she said.

"I just tried to!"

"Yeah, only when something's wrong. And you took Shannon's side on the beach back there, and then you totally spaced out while I was talking to you - it's like you don't even care about me anymore."

"What sides?" he asked, "All I said was we were all ready to leave." Dragging a hand through his hair, he scented the salt from the waves, and wished he were back in the water. The trees were towering, making him feel claustrophobic. He'd felt the rift between him and Sonya, but he didn't want to have an argument. "Can we not do this now? We're standing on a little island, in the middle of the Bahamas. A literal paradise with our friends."

"*Your* friends," she mumbled, looking away from him.

"What does that even mean?" he asked, stepping back from her.

"It means I'm always alone!" she shouted, and slapped her hand over her mouth, shocked at what had slipped out. She backed away from him, eyes wide, before turning and sprinting into the trees.

"Sonya!" Tai shouted, looking up to the path to where their friends had disappeared around a curve. Remembering Rob's warning about people getting lost, he started into the trees. He saw a shadow of her black hair ahead and ran a little faster. Minutes later, he stopped to listen. At first he heard nothing, and saw little through the trees - and the low fog that had come in. "Sonya?" he asked, although his voice sounded dim and muted, even to his own ears. All around him the trees looked the same; tall, where he couldn't even see the tops of them, and eerily similar. No wonder people got lost here, he thought uneasily.

He gazed up, looking into the canopy. Whispers crashed in to fill the silence, and the surfboard slipped from his fingers, forgotten. Like the roaring of a wave, it was everywhere. Thousands of low voices, murmuring; whispering; he couldn't differentiate any voices, or words. Not at first. He closed his eyes, struggling to hear - maybe one of the voices was Sonya's.

Don't be afraid. Tai startled and bumped into a tree, hearing one whisper clearly.

You're safe here. Stay.

Opening his eyes, he whirled around to see the fog had become more dense, and the trees continued to sway. He was winded, as though he'd been running, and called out in a voice unlike his own "Who's there?"

We're here, he heard - from all around him. *We've always been here.* Tai lunged behind trees, but whether he was searching anymore or hiding, he wasn't sure. Searching… what had he been searching for? His friends, maybe. Maybe the voices were his friends, playing a trick on him. James, and… and the other ones.

"Guys? Is that you?" Tai called out, but his voice only came out in a low, breathy tone.

We're here, the voice reassured, *we'll never leave you. Don't leave. Isn't it beautiful here?*

It really was beautiful, Tai thought, nodding and stepping out from behind another tree. He wandered forward in a daze. Colors melded together, all varying hues of greys and blues and browns. There was no trail to follow, so he shuffled between the trees, staring into the canopy of branches. Fog rose from the ground to meet him, tasting his skin. It felt cool but not unpleasant, and smelled of the sea. The scent brought a flashing image - brilliant blue waters, glinting in the sunlight. His fingers flexed, searching for a vivid yellow board he'd forgotten about. Taking a deep breath and shaking his head, Tai stumbled.

The fog lifted, both from around him and within him, and he whipped his head back and forth, searching for... what *had* he been looking for? He closed his eyes and brought back to mind that scene of the beach. Clarity hit with the blunt end of reality, and he remembered Sonya, running away from him into the trees. *These* trees - where the canopy created a permanent twilight, and whispers told people to stay. He broke into a slow jog, keeping the image of Sonya in his mind. In response, the fog thinned, allowing him to see farther. It felt like he jogged for hours... but that couldn't be. The island wasn't even that big, he reasoned. It was just the shadows playing tricks on him.

Her bright pink toenails were the first thing he saw, because he nearly ran into them face-first. Instinct had him jerking to the side to avoid a collision, stumbling into a tree as he stopped. Relief mingled with confusion as he caught his breath; Sonya, never the outdoorsy type, had run into the woods and climbed a tree? With a half grin, he looked up - and saw that she wasn't on any branch. She hadn't climbed any of the trees. Instead, her body swayed back and forth, and her face had turned the color of the trees around them. She was shades of blue and grey. Her shoulders slumped forward, and her head sat heavily to the side. Tai fell to his knees, unable to look away until he finally turned to retch at the base of the tree.

When he turned back to Sonya, he saw the rope she hung from had drawn her higher. Tears made tracks down his face as he knelt, willing her to move. He needed her to make a joke. To yell at him again; to do *anything*. Higher she rose, until he could barely make out her face. It seemed worse somehow, that she was swaying. Death was supposed to mean not moving. His gaze drifted from her lifeless body into the treetops, where he could now make out others. What he had taken as swaying boughs were swaying bodies. Horror ran through him; a reckless child with scissors cutting him from the inside out. The world went back to greys and browns as he surrendered to shock and despair.

It's peaceful, the voice insisted. *No more sorrow, no more pain.*

Tai shook his head. He didn't want to hear this. He couldn't help Sonya; looking up, he couldn't even tell which of the hanging bodies *was* Sonya anymore. As the fog gathered again, reminding him he was all alone, he turned blindly and started walking. The whispers left him alone for a time, until he thought he heard the crashing of the surf, and turned in that direction. They picked up in volume and insistence, slowly poking holes in his reasoning -and his sanity- as he spoke out loud.

"I don't want to be here," he said quietly.

No one wants to be here. We can help you leave.

"I have a life."

Not really, the whispers reasoned, *you're all alone. You couldn't help her, you can't help anyone. We can help you.*

Tai stubbornly set his chin and kept walking forward. He vaguely wondered what time it was. It felt like he'd been walking for days, but the low light hadn't really changed, filtering through the trees-*bodies*, his mind corrected, and he grit his teeth. There had to be a way out…but he was getting so tired. He was afraid if he stopped moving, he'd never get back up. "I don't need help."

*Poor thing, you're so lost. So lost. So lost. So lost. **So lost.***

Although they were still whispers, now there were thousands reminding him he was lost. ***So lost. So lost.*** It reverberated through his head, until tears ran down his face, and his breath was heaving. He stopped and braced against a tree, resting his forehead against the smooth bark. He didn't know what he was fighting for anymore. With a broken sigh, he turned and leaned his back against the tree, closing his eyes.

Poor thing. You need rest. Tai nodded; his heart felt terribly heavy in his chest, weighing him down. There was nothing left. He heard a slithering, and couldn't even find the fear to open his eyes and look for a snake.

Just one more step, encouraged the whispers, *and you'll be free. Rest, little one. It's beautiful here.*

Tai opened his eyes to see a single rope hanging in front of him, tied with a large hole on the end. A noose, he realized. "I don't want to die," he managed, staring at the noose.

But why would you want to live, asked the whispers. Tai didn't have an answer anymore. He felt dead inside already - numb. What was the difference? With a shaky breath, he stepped up to the noose and held it wide.

Almost there, said the whispers, *you're almost done.* So soothing, he thought; killing himself was almost relaxing. Wait, he was about to kill himself? He shook his head and stepped back, holding the rope away from him.

It's just rest. You're so tired. The fog seemed to hug him more closely, making him feel like he was in a large blanket.

His eyes drooped. Yes, he was tired. Lost, and alone, and so horribly exhausted, body and soul. The rope gently came towards him, so that fitting it over his head was smooth. He was adjusting it over his Adam's apple as the whispers asked *Are you ready to fly, little one?*

He nodded, and as the rope slowly pulled tighter, he remembered the feeling of flying. Only he was inside a wave, with water thundering all around, and the sun was making diamonds off the water. For just a moment he could feel the spray and taste the ocean, and Tai kept his hands inside the noose. With a surge of adrenaline, he jumped and pulled at the rope, widening the slip for his head to pass back through.

Peace! You will have peace! The whispers screamed, and dropping to the ground Tai took a gasping breath. He stood, keeping a hand at his neck, and strode forward.

The fog rose to wind around him, and he thought of sunlight. The whispers spoke soothingly of solitude and rest, and he remembered laughter. When he became tired and his legs heavy, he forced himself to pick up his pace. Eventually the voices and fog receded, and he felt almost like he was in a normal forest. He wanted, so badly, to lie down and close his eyes, but he was terrified he wouldn't open them again. So he ran through memories in his head, from holidays and friends to family, and hummed songs when he thought of them.

He recalled being twelve and taking his bike too fast over a jump, and the hospital visit with a broken wrist. His father, showing him how to swim *with* the ocean, instead of against it. If he thought of Sonya at all it was only to picture her laughing - dancing, in a tiny dress and high heels, and singing along to music that was too loud.

The space between trees gradually widened, and the air slowly started to smell like things other than death. Tai smelled the ocean, and took a deep, cleansing breath. At the first birdsong he heard, he smiled.

He came to a low wall covered by planks - the path! He remembered his friends, and how they must be worried sick about him by now. His mood took a plummet as he thought of what to tell them about Sonya. Nothing, he decided. He ran after her, then got lost, that was it. No one would believe him anyway, about... that. Looking behind him into the trees, he watched fog lap at the bases of trees, eager for him to go back. With his heart thudding heavily, he climbed back onto the planks, and walked along the rail until he could see lights up ahead.

A wall with oversized windows let him see into what he figured must be the deli-shop they had been headed to, what seemed like ages ago. Before being in the trees, he would have thought it strange to have such a place in the middle of the woods on a little island. Tai knew his personal gauge for strange was forever changed... *he* was changed.

An older, dark-skinned man stood behind the counter, and watched him come up the path. Tai caught his own reflection in the door before he opened it, and paused in surprise. His cheeks were sunken in; he had dark bags beneath his eyes, and his hair curled down to his shoulders in wild disarray. Most surprisingly there was a streak of white hair running next to his left temple. The older man nodded and smiled very slightly when Tai stepped in. A long moment of silence stretched between the two of them that Tai couldn't decipher until he spoke.

"Not many make it."

Tai froze, and felt the blood rush from his head. "What?"

"Your friends were looking for you."

The man's eyes shifted from Tai to the wall beside the door, where there were several posters and ads; a community board. As he stepped forward, two flyers caught his attention, although they were crowded in by others; one was for a young girl Sonya, with long black hair, last seen wearing a pink bikini. Tai saw in his mind's eye her pretty polished toenails, rising into the grey. The second was of him, pictured on the beach, grinning. With the surreal feeling of a dream, Tai took his own missing persons poster down, and looked back at the man.

"How long?"

The man pursed his lips, and looked back to the trees for a long minute before answering. "Almost two years now."

Still holding tight to the poster, Tai managed to make it to a chair before he collapsed at a low table. The man said nothing, and Tai stayed lost in thought before being startled when the man set down a sandwich and large water in front of him.

"They waited to go in after you," he said, taking the seat across the table and staring into the trees. "The police talked them out of it, told them people get lost here every year. Told them about the sinkholes in these woods."

"We weren't lost," Tai managed. "There are no sinkholes."

The man looked at him a long minute. "I know." He shrugged. "People don't understand it, but they try to make sense of it. They have to explain it somehow. Those kids camped out on that beach for weeks." He leaned forward. "They were good people. I've seen a lot of people come through here, and most can't wait to leave. They were about to give up I think, until a local boy Rob Reyes found his missing surfboard washed up on the beach out behind those trees. They insisted you were alive, they said they could hear you calling, and they were going in."

Tai ignored the sandwich. His stomach cramped at the very idea of food, but he sipped the water. He had to ask.

"Did they make it out?"

The man shook his head, and Tai felt his nausea rise like the tide. He looked to the trees, which held on to their peculiar twilight.

The little man followed his gaze, staring off into the distance. He spoke so low it was almost to himself. Tai had to lean forward to hear.

"The locals say it is no coincidence that there is little difference between the copse and the corpse."

About the Author

Kasey grew up along the East Coast, from Maine to North Carolina. She loves two things above all in nature: the water, and the forest. While she might not love her nightmares, they do inspire many of her works.

She and her dog can be found investigating hiking trails, or curled up together on the couch as he nudges her computer off her lap to make room for himself.

Visit Kasey Fallon online

Use the QR code to see the Author
Fallon website and sign up for
Kasey's free monthly newsletter,
The Foreword, for poetry, book
recommendations and more!

Instagram:
@writ_fallon

Facebook:
Kasey Fallon

The Home
Kasey Fallon

A town almost forgotten; perhaps it should have been.

The Home for Us – now just known as The Home by the locals. Once it belonged to some corporation or other that no one remembers the name of, conducting tests no one spoke of and giving refuge to the undesirables about town. No one asked questions when some of those…individuals quietly left town.

Once the corporation moved on, The Home stood empty; no one quite recalls how it happened, or exactly where those people went.

Still flying flags, using the post office and living their respectable lives, the town is *mostly* supportive when Dr. Christina Devin comes to turn The Home into an addiction treatment center. Maybe it would revive the town a bit.

It's about time this town got some new blood – *and blood is just what they'll get.*

The Home, 1993

Trails of smoke drifted upward in the foyer of the old building as the black cat squeezed its way through the slightly open window. Interested in discovery, she followed the acrid smell and the only source of light in the building, only to be completely unimpressed to find the human behind the desk. Displaying her unquestionable disinterest, she sat and groomed as the human puffed on.

Mrs. Giovanna Antionette Williams had married in the fifties at age sixteen for lust, left her family behind for the promise of riches, and fell from grace in Chicago. Left broke and widowed after that cheating liar had gotten his richly earned heart attack, she started from nothing on the streets of Chicago.

Scrubbing johns in a Chicago hospital wasn't nothing to joke about, she thought, deeply inhaling from her long cigarette. But since scrubbing johns was better than havin'em, it kept her off the streets. It kept her out of trouble, mostly, but she never could get rid of that wild edge to do *more - be more.* Sleeping with a few of the higher-ups in the hospital had given her a leg up - so to put it - in the nursing program, which she found exciting at first but bored of within a year. Only one thing kept her from moving on from nursing - a big to-do came out about the new discoveries in psychology.

Taking another pull and gazing around The Home's foyer, she remembered the buzz. New up-and-coming doctors, new studies, new projects, even new words were being tossed around: *skitzo, psychotics, neurochemistry, antipsychotics and electro-therapy.* She'd stayed to intern on a new project - one that had changed her life.

For thirty years she'd stayed in the middle of godforsaken Oklahoma and spent her life on the cause. For research, maybe, but mostly for herself. Lightly fingering the "retirement" check in her pocket, she chuckled at the amount - justly earned - and knew she'd done damn well for herself. She'd kept her mouth shut for decades, done what she was told and had been rewarded, time and time again.

Lips pursed, she let out a trail of smoke as she searched the large front desk for anything left that would lead anywhere. No bills, no forwarding address, no contacts, no records with names, nothing of any relevance was to be left behind. As she flipped through another drawer, a thud from up the east stairs had her looking up. Holding a number of envelopes from the desk, she called out, mostly out of habit "Dr. Forrester?" A heavy silence met her peering into the darkness. "Sir?"

With no response, Mrs. Williams stubbed out her cigarette and heaved her ample girth from behind the desk. As she stepped forward she clearly recalled watching Dr. Forrester and his newest wife be driven away by their chauffeur over an hour ago. *Was there any other staff who might still - ?*

"Who's there?" she called, more demanding than before. The hairs on the back of her neck stood up, but as she cast her eyes about the room she blamed it on too many windows and the encroaching winter. A soft whisper of sound from the other side of the desk made her peer back around the edge to see a black tail making its way back into the darkness, away from the lamp's circle of light.

Letting out a huff, she shakily picked up her pack from the desk and lit another smoke, drawing deep. *I must be tired to be afraid of Luna.* She would never consider herself a superstitious woman, but she steered well clear of black cats. Luna had been named by their receptionist after wandering onto the grounds one day. Miss Theresa, she recalled, loved all animals. A pet for companionship was fine, she supposed, but she'd never been one for getting fur all over her.

Although she'd never admit out loud exactly why she couldn't stand black cats - or cats in general, really, she shooed the wanderer away now and considered as she sat back down with a sigh.

She supposed cats reminded her too much of the old days - the early days of The Home. When most of them lived by night, lived in secret and were young enough not to be afraid of anything. But Giovanna - Vanna to her friends, if she'd had any - knew too well there was plenty to be afraid of. Things to fear in the dark; things to fear right there in Line Ridge.

Keeping in tune with her morbid thoughts, she figured it was perfect timing when the desk lamp in front of her went dark. Perfect timing to get right on out of here, and keep on moving. She knew sometimes things like that happened here; people would close a door only to have it open moments later, or forget to turn off a light, come back and it was already off. The patients had thought the place was haunted, and they'd lost some staff over it here or there. But she knew better. After pulling the little chain for the lamp twice, her hands felt around the shadowed desk for her cigarettes and purse.

People were forgetful or mistaken was all, she reminded herself as she hastily shrugged into her jacket. Tonight was a perfect example. Hadn't she *told* Miss Theresa that the electric was to be cut the following day? Yet here she was, closing up in the dark, with a cat that should never have been there in the first place.

Studiously ignoring her rattling keys as her hands shook, she made doubly sure the front door was locked tight, deadbolt and all. She hesitated only a moment as she remembered Luna was still inside. *Not her problem; the damn thing probably had fleas anyway.* Wishing for her cigarette, she turned from the door and speed walked down the gravel drive to her waiting car - *staying warm in the cold was all.*

She didn't wait until her car warmed up, though she knew she should have since her Betsy Blue was almost twelve now. Flipping on her headlights, she was startled to see Luna sitting on the front porch, staring after her, with the headlights turning her eyes into glass. She let out a slow breath and put Betsy in gear, not caring if she kicked some gravel loose on her way. By the time she reached the gate at the end of the lumbering driveway she had another cigarette lit and the radio up loud. With her car in park just beyond the gate, she dutifully pulled at the stubborn, squealing metal as the hinges protested. *Miss Theresa should have seen to these, dammit.* As she pulled and twisted, something in her peripheral vision caught her eye - Giovanna felt a slick chill sneak down her spine as she took in a lit window on the third floor of the old mansion.

She took a single step towards the building, her thoughts a riot: *Someone had been in there with her...the lamp...the electric wasn't turned off...the cat... Who...?*

The single light flicked out, as if it knew it had been seen. In five running steps she was back at her car, and another few seconds later Betsy Blue was hitting her max RPMs as she careened onto the main road leading to the highway. Chain smoking by the time she reached the edge of town, she'd convinced herself the gates didn't matter; no one was going to come up that drive except the postman, and that nosy fool deserved whatever waited for him.

Michael Gil would never be considered a timid man, by personality or stature. His mere size as he carried Line Ridge's post day after day could have easily made him a sports star if it weren't for his incredibly sweet nature and opposition to violence. As the only full-time postman in town he knew nearly all of the residents, and enjoyed getting to know each of their families and quirks.

He was the first to know when who was having a baby; the first deliverer of gifts leading up to Christmas; the bearer of news, both good and bad. His wife Antonia secretly wished he weren't *quite* so involved in the town. She figured he spent more time gossiping than she did. Michael of course would have been appalled to hear his passion boiled down to *gossip* - it was part of his job after all.

With a hobby shed at the back of the house, a golden retriever who loved running despite a bit of hip dysplasia at her ripe age of eight, a wife who enjoyed her own day job out of town and the thorough enjoyment he got from working for the Post Office, Michael considered his life a sight close to perfect...except maybe, for The Home.

Every day -rain or shine, wind or snow- he brought the mail to each residence and most businesses in town, often preferring to walk, and he left The Home for last. The grounds were situated on the far east edge of town, on the other side of Sal's old pond but before the train tracks. Between the distance and the driveway being longer than a football field he was forced to drive, but seeing as that got him to and away from the place quicker, Michael didn't mind.

It sat alone on the property aside from a decrepit woodshed at the rear. There was a rumor back when Michael was in high school that partiers would drink and smoke there; whether Michael ever attended he never told his wife, but she knew for a fact he hated the place. He hated the archaic, gothic look of the stone mansion, its girth spreading out endlessly; hated the old wrought iron fence that was now frozen open, but he remembered clearly when it used to squeal its way shut, closing folks in and their loved ones out.

Delivering mail was easier here several years back… when there were more people around to chat with and distract him from the rows and rows of darkened windows staring at him. Now, as he stepped out of his mail truck with a sigh and gazed around, it greeted him as it had become; haunted. The grey sky as a backdrop and the caws of crows certainly didn't help his anxiety as he hummed a Christmas tune, trying in vain to block them out.

As eerie as The Home was at that moment, he was oddly relieved that the recent buzz had died down some. These last few weeks there had been… what he supposed he'd call a restlessness about the place. A few people about, but no one willing to talk or even look him in the eye. He'd seen three large vans had been parked out back but when he'd delivered last week and asked about them (as *any* friendly person would, he was sure) he was given a distinct non-answer, "Just moving ..things around," with a tight smile from Theresa at the front desk as her eyes wandered around the desk between them.

The general quiet and the crows accompanied him up the grand stone steps. Crossing the wide expanse of the front porch, his brow creased as he looked through the front door into… the dark. No lights. Not even a lowly desk lamp highlighted the encroaching darkness as the sun set. No one sat behind the welcome desk or came to the door to fetch the mail. Michael tried the door and although the antique handle pivoted downward, there was no give; someone had set the deadbolt.

His confused expression in the reflection of the window stared back at him as he tried again peering into the foyer, knocking. No one ever came.